Avalanche! Road Closed!

"All right, no need to panic." Mr. Samuels said loudly. "Has anyone headed out to the lifts yet? No? Good. We're not really in avalanche territory, but we'd better close down the south side trails just in case. Everyone stick to the trails marked in green."

Eddie raised his hand. "What about the bunny slope?"

Mr. Samuels smiled. "That's perfectly safe," he said. "I can guarantee there won't be an avalanche there."

"But how are we going to get out of here this afternoon?" an adult asked, sounding anxious.

"You can't," Henry said. "That highway is the only way down the mountain. We're all stranded until they dig it out. That might not be until tomorrow."

Join the CLUE CREW
& solve these other cases!

NANCY DREW

#11 AND THE CLUE CREW™

Ski School Sneak

BY CAROLYN KEENE

ILLUSTRATED BY MACKY PAMINTUAN

Aladdin Paperbacks
New York London Toronto Sydney

This book is a work of fiction. Any references to historical events, real people, or real locales are used fictitiously. Other names, characters, places, and incidents are the product of the author's imagination, and any resemblance to actual events or locales or persons, living or dead, is entirely coincidental.

6☞ ALADDIN PAPERBACKS

An imprint of Simon & Schuster Children's Publishing Division

1230 Avenue of the Americas, New York, NY 10020

Text copyright © 2007 by Simon & Schuster, Inc.

Illustrations copyright © 2007 by Macky Pamintuan

All rights reserved, including the right of reproduction in whole or in part in any form.

NANCY DREW AND THE CLUE CREW is a trademark of Simon & Schuster, Inc.

NANCY DREW, ALADDIN PAPERBACKS, and related logo are registered trademarks of Simon & Schuster, Inc.

Designed by Lisa Vega.

The text of this book was set in ITC Stone Informal.

Manufactured in the United States of America

First Aladdin Paperbacks edition November 2007

10 9

Library of Congress Control Number 2007927236

ISBN-13: 978-1-4169-4936-7

ISBN-10: 1-4169-4936-4

0212 OFF

CONTENTS

Ski School Sneak

ChAPTER ONE

Fun on the Slopes

"Look out below!"

Nancy Drew looked up just in time to see her friend George Fayne skidding down the snowy hill—straight at her. Unfortunately, she couldn't get out of the way fast enough. It was hard to move quickly while wearing skis!

"Aaaah!" Nancy cried as George crashed into her. Both girls fell and slid down the gentle slope. Nancy felt cold snow going into the collar of her red coat.

They slid to a stop at the bottom of the hill. George sat up and brushed off her down jacket. She took off her ski helmet and shook snow out of her short, dark hair.

"Sorry, Nancy," she said breathlessly.

"What happened this time?" Nancy asked with a smile. "Did the wind blow you off course again?"

It was a warm but windy winter day at Mount Fun Ski Lodge. George, Nancy, and their other best friend, Bess Marvin, who was also George's cousin, had come to Mount Fun with George's parents. All three girls were eight years old and lived in River Heights, about two hours' drive from Mount Fun.

"It wasn't the wind this time," George said. "Two raccoons were playing in the woods near the top of the hill. They were really cute. I guess I got distracted by watching them and forgot to pay attention to my skiing."

A young woman in a green jacket skied over. Her name was Margie, and she was one of the ski instructors watching over the bunny slope. That was what they called the wide, gentle hill near the lodge. People could learn to ski there and practice until they were good enough to tackle

the bigger, scarier trails farther up the mountain.

"Are you girls okay?" Margie asked. "That was quite a spill."

"I'm fine," George said. "Luckily, Nancy was there to break my fall."

Nancy laughed. "I'm fine too, Margie. Just a little snowy."

Margie gave them a thumbs-up, then skied

off. Nancy noticed that a couple of other instructors were watching them. So were a bunch of other kids. When she and George untangled their skis and poles from each other and stood up, the kids laughed and cheered. George grinned and took a bow.

"Oh well," Nancy said. "I guess neither of us will win that award for Best New Skier that Mr. Samuels was talking about!"

Mr. Samuels was the owner of Mount Fun. He'd announced that he would give out a few awards at lunchtime. One would go to the best first-time skier on the bunny slope.

"Hey! Are you guys okay?" Bess skied down the hill toward her friends, her blond hair streaming out from under her pink helmet.

Bess came to an expert stop by turning the toes of her skis in. Nancy was impressed. None of the three girls had ever skied before that morning, when they had all taken their very first beginner ski class. But Bess was definitely catching on fast.

"We're fine," Nancy said. "George got distracted by some raccoons."

Bess giggled. "We're supposed to be skiing, not watching raccoons." She looked up at the busy bunny slope. "This is fun, isn't it?"

The slope was filled with kids of all ages. It was Mount Fun's first ever Half-Price Kids Weekend, and lots of families had come to take advantage of the bargain.

"It's awesome." Nancy grinned as George tried to dump snow out of her mitten. "But what do you think, George? That was, like, the tenth time you came down the hill on your rear end!"

"That's okay," George said. "I'd rather be here falling in the snow with you guys than stuck at some stupid car race with my brothers."

George's two brothers were at a big car race with their grandparents. George's parents didn't like car racing, so they'd offered to take George and her friends skiing instead. Mr. and Mrs. Fayne were trying some of the harder trails while the girls stayed on the bunny slope under the watchful eye of the ski instructors.

"I'm starving," George said. "I think I'll go get the rest of my breakfast bar. It's in my backpack."

"Can't you wait?" Bess asked her cousin. "Lunch starts in . . ." She pushed back the sleeve of her jacket. As always, she was wearing her special watch that told the time all over the world. "Fifty-seven minutes," she finished.

"That's fifty-seven minutes too long. Especially when I have half a breakfast bar waiting for me." George licked her lips and headed across the flat area at the bottom of the bunny slope.

Nancy and Bess followed. Nancy was feeling a little hungry too. Skiing was hard work! But she didn't mind waiting for lunch. Besides, she'd eaten her whole breakfast bar on the ride to Mount Fun that morning.

Soon they reached the equipment shed. It was a small, brightly painted building where people could rent skis, boots, helmets, and other equipment. There was a long line of benches in front where skiers could sit to adjust their boots and put on their skis. Right now the benches were covered with backpacks, shoes, and other belongings. Off to one side, a covered walkway led to the cedar-shingled main lodge building.

"Hey, who knocked my backpack on the ground?" George grumbled. She grabbed it and felt around inside. "And who took my breakfast bar?" she cried. "It's not here!"

"Uh-oh!" Bess said with a laugh. "Sounds like a mystery for the Clue Crew!"

Nancy grinned. She and her friends loved solving mysteries, so they had started a club called the Clue Crew.

"Don't bother to start investigating," Nancy said. "I've already solved the mystery."

She pointed to a large, shaggy dog a few yards away. He had something in his mouth, and his tail was wagging.

"Blizzard!" George cried. "You stole my breakfast bar!"

Nancy and her friends had met Blizzard soon after their arrival at Mount Fun. He was the lodge owner's dog and the official mascot of the slopes. He was very friendly, and loved kids.

"We should get it away from him before he eats the plastic wrapping," Nancy said.

"Here, Blizzard," Bess cooed. "Good dog."

Blizzard was so excited to see her that he dropped what was in his mouth and licked her face. Bess reached down and grabbed the remains of George's breakfast bar. She dumped it in a nearby trash can, then wrinkled her nose.

"Ew, Blizzard slimed my new mitten." Bess peeled off one blue mitten and shook it. Dog slobber and granola crumbs went flying.

"At least your mitten will dry,"

George said sadly. "What about my breakfast bar?"

"Don't worry." Bess checked her watch again. "Now there's only fifty minutes until lunch."

"Sounds like just enough time to do some more skiing!" Nancy said.

Soon the three girls were waiting in line for the rope pull, a mechanized rope and pulley that towed skiers up to the top of the bunny slope. Nancy was behind a boy named Jack. He had been in their beginner ski class that morning.

"Hi," she greeted him as they both grabbed on to the rope. "How's it going?"

"Great," Jack said. "I'm really good at skiing. I'll win that new skier award for sure."

"Really?" Nancy said politely.

"Yup." Jack looked proud. "I'm great at most sports. Last summer, when my family rented a lake house, I learned to water ski in, like, ten minutes. I'm the best player on my soccer team too."

"That's nice," Nancy said. When Jack wasn't looking, she rolled her eyes at Bess and George. She could tell they thought Jack's bragging was obnoxious too.

She forgot about Jack when they reached the top. Even though she'd skied down the bunny slope at least fifteen times that day, Nancy still felt nervous looking down the hill.

"Ready?" Bess asked, lifting her poles. She didn't sound nervous at all. "Let's go!"

She pushed off. George glanced at Nancy and shrugged. "Here goes nothing," George said. "I'll go first. That way at least I won't run into you again."

"Thanks." Nancy smiled and watched George push off. Then she took a deep breath and followed.

The air whistled

past her ears as she picked up speed. Thinking back to her morning ski class, she bent her knees and turned, slowing her speed a little. Soon she was swooping back and forth almost as expertly as Bess. By the time she reached the bottom, she was grinning from ear to ear. Skiing was fun!

She skied over to Bess and George, who were standing by Margie. "Good job, Nancy," the ski instructor said. "That looked a lot better than your last trip!" She winked at George. "Both of you stayed upright this time."

Nancy and George laughed. "It felt a lot better too," George said. "Skiing on your backside isn't that much fun."

Margie chuckled. "You'll get the hang of it. Just watch how your friend here does it." She patted Bess on the shoulder. "Before long, she'll be ready to try the regular slopes!"

Out of the corner of her eye, Nancy saw Jack sliding to a stop nearby. He was staring at Bess with a frown. Nancy guessed he'd heard what Margie had said to Bess and was upset that she hadn't said it about him instead.

Serves him right for all that bragging, Nancy thought.

"Heads up!" someone screamed suddenly.

Nancy spun around. A skier was careening down the slope at breakneck speed—heading straight toward them!

ChaPTER TWo

Crashers and Complainers

"Look out!" Margie cried. She pushed the girls out of the way. A second later the runaway skier flew past them. He fell on the flat ground at the bottom of the hill and skidded along on his side. He finally crashed to a stop in a pile of snow.

"Whew! That was close," George said.

"Everyone okay here?" Margie asked. The girls nodded, and the instructor hurried off toward the runaway skier.

"Who *was* that?" Nancy wondered.

Jack skied over. "I think it's that kid Eddie from our ski class," he said. "Remember? He tried to put his skis on backward, then tripped over his poles, like, three times in the first five minutes."

Nancy remembered Eddie. He was a tall, gangly kid around her age. He did seem kind of clumsy. But he also seemed nice—a lot nicer than Jack, anyway.

She saw Margie helping Eddie to his feet. Blizzard went trotting toward them, and Eddie leaned over to pat the dog. But he forgot he was wearing skis, and managed to fall down again.

Jack snorted as he watched. "That kid should be banned from the slopes," he said. "He's a safety hazard. Especially to himself!"

"That's not very nice," Bess told Jack with a frown.

Jack smirked. "Maybe not. But it's true."

By now Eddie was on his feet again. He came toward the girls and Jack with Margie helping him along. "Sorry about that," he called breathlessly. "I didn't mean to scare you guys. I guess I'm not too great at skiing yet."

"No duh," Jack muttered.

Margie shot Jack a stern look. "That's okay," she told Eddie. "I'm sure you'll get the hang of it sooner or later."

"Later," Jack said. "Definitely later." He dug his poles into the snow and skied off toward the rope pull.

"What a jerk," George said, watching him go.

Eddie sighed. "No, he's right," he said. "Maybe this just isn't for me."

He waved one arm to help make his point. But he forgot he was holding his ski pole, and it almost bonked Nancy in the head. She ducked just in time.

"Oops!" Eddie's cheeks turned red. "Sorry about that."

Margie chuckled. "Hey, at least she was wearing a helmet!"

Nancy smiled and nodded. She could tell Margie was trying to make Eddie feel better.

"I'd better go find my friend Steve," Eddie said. "He's skiing on the regular slopes with his dad. We're supposed to meet before lunch." He moved off, sliding his skis very carefully along the snowy ground.

Nancy noticed that George was fiddling with her ski boots. "I think I busted a buckle when Margie pushed us out of the way," George said. "I can't get it to close."

Margie bent over to see. "Looks like you're right. Just go into the equipment shed and tell Mr. Samuels what happened. He'll get you fixed up with new boots."

The girls headed for the equipment shed. Inside they found the lodge owner sitting on a stool drinking a cup of coffee. Mr. Samuels was a cheerful-looking man with a big mustache.

"What can I do for you ladies?" he asked in

his booming voice. "Here to trade in your skis for a different color?"

Bess giggled. "No, thanks," she said. "I love my blue and white skis. They match my coat and mittens."

"I aim to please." Mr. Samuels smiled. "So are you girls having fun?"

"Definitely!" Nancy said.

George nodded. "I don't know why we never tried skiing before. It's great."

"Well, I don't know why I never tried a Half-Price Kids Weekend before," Mr. Samuels said. "It's terrific having all you kids around yelling and laughing and having fun. Much more interesting than boring old grown-ups."

All three girls giggled. Then George showed Mr. Samuels the problem with her ski boot. He found her a new pair.

"There you go," he said. "Better hurry and get out there. You should have time for a couple more runs before lunch."

The girls headed outside to put their skis back

on. Blizzard was sniffing around hopefully at the backpacks, and Nancy gave him a pat. She stepped back into her skis, then sat down to wait for George to finish putting on her new boots.

A girl was sitting farther down the row of benches talking to a pair of worried-looking adults. She was a few years older than Nancy, with bright red hair and a sour expression on her face.

"Can't we go home early?" she whined. "I'm tired of hanging out in the freezing cold."

Her parents exchanged a glance. "It's not that cold, Gina," her mother said. "The radio said it's one of the warm-est winter days in years."

"I don't care." Gina crossed her arms.

"I'm bored. I hate skiing, and there's nothing else to do here."

She really seems upset, Nancy thought. *But who could be bored in a cool place like this?*

"There's plenty to do," Gina's father said cheerfully. "We're going to have lots of fun this weekend even if you don't want to ski tomorrow. We could go on a nature hike."

"Mr. Samuels says there are all sorts of winter creatures around," Gina's mother agreed.

"Rabbits, deer, raccoons, squirrels . . ."

"Indeed," Gina's father said. "Why, a cute little rabbit ran across my path just a few minutes ago, and I'm sure I spotted deer tracks in the snow at the top of the hill. And look—aren't those raccoon droppings over there near that bush?"

"Ew!" Gina shrieked. "Okay, Dad, you totally convinced me—skiing isn't anywhere near as gross and lame as going around identifying animal poop!"

"Wow," Bess whispered in Nancy's ear. "My mom and dad would so ground me if I talked to them like that."

Meanwhile Gina kicked off her skis and jumped to her feet. "I can't believe you're forcing me to stay here," she cried. "I'd do anything to get back home. Anything!" She burst into tears and raced off.

"What a brat!" George said after Gina's parents had hurried away too.

"Forget her," Bess said. "We only have twenty-two minutes left to ski before lunchtime!"

The girls had time for two more trips up and down the hill before the lunch bell rang. Soon the benches by the equipment shed were crowded with kids taking off their skis. Nancy and her friends changed back into their regular shoes, and stacked their ski equipment neatly inside the shed with everyone else's.

"Could I have your attention, everyone?" Mr. Samuels called out. He was standing in front of the benches with Margie and a couple of the other instructors. "Thanks all of you for helping make our first Half-Price Kids Weekend such a success! Now, I know that some of you will be leaving after lunch, so I want to hand out some awards from the morning session." He held up three shiny gold trophies.

"Wow, those are cool!" George said. "I wish I was a better skier so I could win one."

Mr. Samuels announced the first two winners: Best Under-Six Skier and Best Overall Skier. Then he held up the last trophy.

"This one is for Best New Skier," he said. "That's the person who has never skied before but is learning the fastest. And the winner is— Miss Bess Marvin!"

ChaPTER ThREE

Lunch and a Surprise

Nancy and George cheered loudly as Bess stepped forward to accept her award. Most of the other kids clapped too. The only one who looked unhappy was Jack. He was scowling and staring at the ground.

"Check out the spoilsport," George whispered, nudging Nancy.

"I saw," Nancy whispered back. "I guess he really thought that trophy was his."

When Bess returned, Nancy and George gave her a hug. "You're the best," Nancy told her. "We always knew it."

"Thanks." Bess grinned. "Come on, let's go

to lunch. All this trophy winning makes me hungry!"

They headed for the walkway to the lodge. On the way, they passed Jack.

"Hey." George smirked at him. "Did you see Bess's trophy?"

"It should be *my* trophy." Jack glared at Bess. "Mr. Samuels made a big mistake. He'll see!"

George rolled her eyes. "Don't be such a sore loser," she said.

Jack stomped away without answering. The girls shrugged and headed inside.

The lodge dining room was set up family style, with guests sharing several long tables. A delicious selection of soups, sandwiches, and other tasty items was set out on a buffet table at one end of the room. The girls found George's parents chatting with several other adults and a group of older teenagers at one of the tables.

As the girls ate, Nancy watched for Eddie, hoping he and his friends would arrive in time to claim the last three spots at their table. But before he could appear, Gina and her parents walked over and sat down.

"Ugh," George whispered to Nancy. "Figures we get stuck with Miss Prissypants."

George's parents and the other adults were already exchanging introductions with Gina's parents. Meanwhile Bess smiled at Gina.

"Hi, I'm Bess," she said. "This is Nancy, and that's George."

"George?" Gina repeated. She hung her coat on her chair. "Is that really your name? You look like a girl."

"I am a girl," George said. "It's a nickname." She didn't tell Gina her real name, which was Georgia. She hated when people called her that.

Gina didn't seem very interested, anyway. She stared at her plate. "This food is gross," she complained. "I wish I was at home eating something decent."

Nancy picked up her sandwich and took a big bite. "I think it tastes great," she said. Normally she didn't talk with her mouth full.

But she was getting tired of Gina's complaining.

Gina turned to her mother. "My stomach hurts," she announced. "Can we go home now?"

"That's enough, Gina," her mother said sharply. "Can't we just eat lunch in peace?"

"Fine!" Gina jumped up, pushing back her chair so sharply that her coat fell to the floor. "If anyone needs me, I'll be in the bathroom being miserable all by myself."

She flounced off in the direction of the restrooms. Gina's mother started to stand up, but Gina's father put out a hand to stop her.

"Let her go, dear," he said quietly. He picked up Gina's coat and hung it back on her chair. "Just give her time. She's only acting up because she's disappointed."

Nancy wondered what he meant. It sounded kind of mysterious. She glanced at her friends, but they hadn't heard him.

Then she smiled at herself. She was here to ski, not to look for mysteries.

"Hey, Bess," she said. "When we go back

outside, will you help me practice that stop you were doing earlier?"

The girls spent the next few minutes chatting about skiing. They were all on their second helpings of lunch when they saw Eddie walking toward them holding a steaming mug.

"Hi! Where are you sitting?" Bess asked him.

"With Steve and his dad," Eddie said. "They're right over th—Oops!"

When he moved his arm to point to the next table, he accidentally tipped his mug. A blob of whipped cream and a dribble of hot chocolate landed on the shoulder of Bess's sweater.

"Oh, gosh! I'm sorry!" Eddie cried, looking horrified.

"No big deal," Bess said. "I'll clean it off in the bathroom."

Eddie still looked worried. "Are you sure?"

"Totally." Bess smiled at him. "Don't worry about it."

"Okay. Sorry again. See you guys after lunch." Eddie hurried off.

Bess stood up. "I'll be right back." After telling Mrs. Fayne where she was going, she headed for the restrooms.

"That Eddie sure is a klutz," George said. "Someday he's going to trip and fall into a pond full of alligators or something."

Nancy laughed. "That's okay. He'd probably end up accidentally poking the alligators in the eye trying to swim back to shore."

Bess returned a few minutes later. The shoulder of her sweater was damp, but you couldn't see the hot chocolate anymore.

"Did cranky Gina help you clean it off?" George joked.

"No." Bess glanced at Gina's empty seat. "Come to think of it, she wasn't in the bathroom. I wonder where she went."

"I don't," George said. "I'm tired of listening to her complain about being forced to spend the whole weekend at Mount Fun. I wish *we* could stay all weekend instead of just today. I'd definitely appreciate it more than that spoiled Gi—Ow!"

She stopped and rubbed her shoulder, glaring at Bess. "Why'd you hit me?" George asked. But Nancy saw what Bess had seen. Gina had finally returned to the table.

"Isn't lunch over yet?" she complained. "Everything here takes forever."

Nancy looked at her watch. Gina had been gone for over twenty minutes. If she hadn't been in the bathroom, where had she gone?

Stop it! she told herself. *No mysteries, remember?*

"Uh-oh," Bess said. "I think I have a mystery for us to solve."

Nancy was surprised. Was Bess reading her mind?

Bess held up one blue mitten. "My other mitten is missing."

George laughed. "That's a tough one," she teased. "We'll have to look for clues to figure out whether you dropped it on your way to the bathroom, or outside while we were changing shoes."

"Don't worry, we'll find it," Nancy said. "It's time to head back outside anyway."

Sure enough, at that moment Mr. Samuels stood up from his seat near the buffet table and wiped his mustache with a napkin. "Everyone ready for more skiing?" he called out. "Let's hit the slopes!"

Cheers rose from all over the room. Nancy and her friends joined the crowd heading for the doors.

"Watch for my mitten," Bess reminded them.

They hadn't spotted it by the time they reached the equipment shed. But Nancy forgot about Bess's mitten when she heard gasps and cries of alarm from inside the shed. As soon as she looked inside, she understood why.

The equipment shed was a huge mess!

CHAPTER FOUR

A Vandal Scandal

"Who could have done this?" someone cried.

"Don't worry," Mr. Samuels said, but he sounded worried himself. "I'm sure there's an explanation. Maybe the wind . . ."

Nancy stared in amazement. There was no way the wind could have made such a mess. Skis were knocked over and lying every which way. Boots were flung everywhere. Helmets and poles lay scattered across the floor.

"Looks like a mystery," Nancy said to her friends. "You know what that means . . ."

"Time for the Clue Crew to get to work!" Bess said, and George nodded.

Nancy hurried outside to get her backpack,

then returned to the shed. She took out the
purple detective notebook she carried with her
everywhere.

"Let's start asking around to see if anyone

saw anything suspicious," she told her friends. Jack was standing nearby staring at the mess. "Hey!" she called to him. "You were sitting at the table by the door, right?" She remembered passing him on the way in to lunch.

"Yeah," Jack said. "So?"

"So you must've been one of the first ones out here," Nancy said. "What did you see when you walked in?"

Jack gave her a strange look. "Why are you being so nosy?"

"I'm just trying to—Hey!" Nancy protested as George yanked on her arm, pulling her aside.

"Careful!" George hissed. "You-know-who could be a suspect." She jerked her head toward Jack.

"Jack?" Nancy shook her head. "I doubt it. I saw him at lunch."

"Were you watching him the whole time?" George asked. "He could have sneaked out here long enough to mess stuff up."

"Why would he do that? He likes skiing,

remember?" Nancy stared at her notebook. "We should list some suspects, though."

"Mr. Samuels thinks it was the wind," Bess said.

Nancy didn't think so, but she wrote *Wind* at the top of the list. "Who else?"

"Blizzard?" George suggested. "Maybe he was looking for more breakfast bars and accidentally made this mess."

"Okay." Nancy wrote the dog's name on the list.

Just then George's father hurried over. "Better find your skis and get out there, girls," he said. "We just heard the weather report in the lobby, and it's supposed to get even windier. I'm afraid we'll have to leave earlier than we planned—the road conditions could get dangerous."

"Bummer!" George exclaimed. "We were planning to ski all afternoon!"

"I know." Mr. Fayne smiled. "Don't worry, we can stay another hour or so. But then we'll have to hit the road."

"Oh well," Nancy said as Mr. Fayne hurried off. "I guess we won't have time to solve this mystery after all."

"That's okay." Bess shrugged. "It was probably Blizzard."

"Probably," Nancy said, though secretly she was a little disappointed. She loved solving mysteries. But she could do that at home. Today was her only chance to ski.

She stuck her notebook in her pocket. Then she and her friends dug through the mess trying to find their skis, boots, helmets, and poles. All around them, other kids were doing the same.

"I found my stuff," George announced, digging into a pile. She pulled out a boot. "Hey Nancy, isn't this yours?"

"Do you see any blue skis?" Bess asked.

Eddie was digging through a different pile nearby. "Did you say blue skis?" he called. "There's a pair of blue and white ones over there—see? It's practically the only set that didn't get messed up."

Nancy looked where he was pointing. Sure enough, a pair of blue skis was leaning against the wall right where Bess had left them.

Jack heard Eddie too. He stared from the blue skis to Bess and back again. "Weird," he said. "How come yours are the only skis that didn't get thrown around?"

"I don't know," Bess said. "Just lucky, I guess."

"Did anyone lose a mitten?" someone called out.

Nancy glanced over and saw an older girl waving a blue mitten in the air. Bess saw it too.

"That's mine!" Bess cried, hurrying over. "Thanks. Where did you find it?"

"Right here in the middle of this big pile of skis," the girl said.

"Weird," Jack said again, staring at Bess. "How would your mitten get under all that stuff?"

"Who cares?" George answered for Bess.

"*I care!*" Jack announced loudly. He turned and pointed straight at Bess. "It was her! Miss Best New Skier. *She* must have wrecked this place!"

CHAPTER FIVE

Accused!

"What?" George shrieked. "Are you crazy?"

Bess gasped. "I didn't do it!" she cried. "I was inside eating lunch with everyone else."

Nancy put her arm around Bess. "We know," she said. "Plus you'd never do something like this."

"Of course you're going to say that," Jack said. "You're her friends. But I saw her leave the lunchroom. She probably sneaked out here then."

"Kids, kids!" Mr. Samuels hurried toward them. "Let's not get ahead of ourselves."

But Nancy noticed he was staring at Bess with a dubious look on his face. Could he really believe Bess might have wrecked the equipment shed?

"Think about it," Jack said. "Her skis weren't messed up. And the mitten proves it."

"Be quiet!" George clenched her fists.

Mr. Fayne came over. "What's going on?" he asked. "Is Bess being accused of something?"

"Not at all," Mr. Samuels said soothingly. "But maybe we should go outside for a private talk. . . ."

Nancy watched worriedly as Mr. Samuels, Mr. Fayne, and Bess went outside. She glanced at Jack, who looked smug.

"Bess didn't do anything wrong," she told him.

"Whatever," Jack said. "I don't really care. I just want to ski."

He hurried off. "What a jerk," George muttered. "Next time I fall down the hill, I'm going to try to fall on him."

Soon Bess and the adults returned. The two men were smiling, but Bess looked anxious.

"All right, everybody, let's forget about this mess and get back to skiing," Mr. Samuels called out cheerfully.

"What happened?" George asked Bess.

Bess shrugged. "Your dad told him I didn't do it," she said. "Mr. Samuels said he believes us."

Nancy could tell Bess was upset about being accused. Kids were shooting Bess looks as they gathered their equipment. Some looked suspicious, and some just looked curious. Nancy was sure they were all thinking the same thing: Did Bess do it?

Bess pulled on her mittens and frowned. "Look!" she cried.

She held up the mitten that had gone missing. Her fingers were visible through a big, ragged hole.

"Oh no!" Nancy exclaimed. "Those are brand-new!"

"It looks like something chewed on it," George said, leaning closer for a better look. "Maybe it was Blizzard looking for crumbs."

Nancy pulled her note-book out of her pocket. "Sounds like a clue."

"I thought we were giving up on the mystery," George said.

"We can't," Nancy said. "Bess's reputation is at stake." Suddenly the mystery seemed much more important than it had a few minutes ago.

"Thanks, you guys," Bess said. "But we still don't have much time. How are we going to figure it out before we leave?"

"The Clue Crew can do anything if we put our minds to it!" George said.

Nancy nodded. "Let's get to work. The first thing we can do is add Jack's name to the sus-pect list."

"Told you so." George looked smug.

"I didn't think he had a motive before," Nancy said. "But now I'm not so sure. Maybe he's hoping Mr. Samuels will take away Bess's trophy and give it to him instead."

Bess's eyes widened. "Do you really think so?"

"Maybe." Nancy chewed on the end of her pencil. "But we shouldn't jump to conclusions. What motives are there for the other suspects?"

George ticked them off on her fingers. "Blizzard's motive is looking for food. The wind's motive is, um, being wind."

"Okay," Nancy said. "Should we—"

Before she could finish, there was a loud crash. Nancy looked over and saw Eddie sprawled on the floor. He had just tripped over a pile of skis.

Bess bit her lip. "Do you think . . ."

"We should make Eddie a suspect?" Nancy finished. "I guess so. He seems nice, but he *is* awfully clumsy."

"But why would he want to mess up the shed?" Bess asked.

"Maybe he came in here for some other reason and did it by accident," George said. "He could be too embarrassed to own up to it."

Nancy added Eddie's name to the suspect list. "Should we try searching the shed?" she asked her friends. "Maybe we'll find more clues, or—"

Once again she was interrupted, this time by a shout from outside.

"*Avalanche!*"

ChaPTER Six

Avalanche!

There was a flurry of shouts and screams. Nancy ran outside with everyone else. An instructor named Henry was out there.

"I just came from the lodge," Henry announced. "There was a big slide down at Winding Pass. The highway is blocked!"

"Oh no!" someone cried.

"Was anyone hurt?" someone else asked.

Henry shook his head. "Luckily traffic is light this time of day," he said. "But they're not sure when it'll be safe to get the equipment in to clear the road. The warm weather combined with the high winds makes it too risky right now."

Nancy exchanged a glance with her friends. She knew that avalanches were very serious. Tons of snow could come loose and slide down the mountain, wiping out everything in its path.

"All right, no need to panic." Mr. Samuels said loudly. "Has anyone headed out to the lifts yet? No? Good. We're not really in avalanche territory, but we'd better close down the south side trails just in case. Everyone stick to the trails marked in green."

Eddie raised his hand. "What about the bunny slope?"

Mr. Samuels smiled. "That's perfectly safe," he said. "I can guarantee there won't be an avalanche there."

"But how are we going to get out of here this afternoon?" an adult asked, sounding anxious.

"You can't," Henry said. "That highway is the only way down the mountain. We're all stranded until they dig it out. That might not be until tomorrow."

"Stranded at Mount Fun!" a teenage boy cried out. "Woo-hoo!"

Several other kids laughed and cheered too. But others, including most of the parents, still looked worried.

"Don't fret," Mr. Samuels said. "We'll find room for everyone at the lodge. Nobody will have to sleep out in the snow with the bears."

That made everyone laugh. "Come on, people," Margie yelled cheerfully. "Let's ski!"

Bess chewed her lower lip. "This stinks," she said. "Now we're stuck here all night with a bunch of people who think I wrecked the shed."

"Look at it this way," Nancy told her. "Now we have all night to solve the mystery."

"Still," Bess said, glancing around. "I wish we could leave today."

Gina walked by just in time to hear her. "What's the big deal?" she complained. "Now you know how I feel being stuck here tonight instead of being home at my friend's birthday party."

She walked on. Nancy looked at her friends. "Did you hear that?" she said. "I think we'd better add Gina to our list."

George nodded. "She could have messed up the shed to try to make her parents leave sooner."

"And she *was* gone from lunch for a long time." Nancy added Gina's name to her notebook. "Let's go question her."

The friends caught up with Gina. The grumpy girl was putting on her ski boots.

"Hi," Nancy said. "Can I ask you something?"

Gina shrugged. "It's a free country." She bent over to adjust her boot.

"You were gone from lunch for a

while," Nancy said. "Where did you go?"

"The bathroom," Gina said. "Just like I said."

"But I went to the bathroom a few minutes later," Bess said. "You weren't there."

Gina sat up and stared at them. "Oh, *I* get it," she said. "You guys are trying to frame me!"

"What?" Nancy said.

"You want to blame me for messing up the skis and stuff." Gina waved a hand at the shed. "You know, so your friend won't get in trouble for what she did." She stared at Bess.

"Bess didn't do anything!" George exclaimed.

"Whatever." Gina rolled her eyes. "Just don't drag me into it."

Nancy led her friends away. "This isn't doing any good," she said. "Let's check out some of the other suspects."

"Whoops!"

The girls looked up just in time to see Eddie go sprawling facedown in the snow nearby. Nancy chewed her lower lip. "Maybe we should talk to Eddie next," she said.

"Do you really think he could have done it?" Bess asked.

"I hope not," Nancy admitted. "But we need to check out every suspect."

They reached Eddie as he climbed back to his feet. "Hi," he greeted them. He brushed snow off his jacket. "Are you guys heading over to the hill?"

"In a minute," Nancy said. "First we want to ask you something."

"What?" Eddie asked.

Nancy took a deep breath. "We didn't see you until lunch was, like, half over," she said. "Were you in the dining room the whole time?"

"Huh?" Eddie's smile faded. Suddenly he looked kind of nervous. "Why would you ask something like that?"

"We were just wondering," George said. "It's kind of weird that we didn't see you."

"That's because it was crowded," Eddie said quickly. "I was there the whole time. Really."

Uh-oh, Nancy thought, her heart sinking. *He definitely seems nervous. Could he be the culprit?*

She couldn't help feeling disappointed. Eddie seemed so nice. He wouldn't let Bess get in trouble because of his clumsiness. Would he?

"Look, Eddie," she said. "We just want to find out the truth. That's all."

Eddie let out a loud sigh. "Okay," he said. "But you have to swear not to tell anyone else."

CHAPTER SEVEN

A New Clue?

Nancy held her breath. Was Eddie about to confess?

"It's my backpack," Eddie said.

"Huh?" George looked confused.

Nancy knew how she felt. What did Eddie's backpack have to do with anything?

"It's lost. That's where I was for the first part of lunch," Eddie explained. "I came out here to look for it. I checked around the benches and over by the rope pull." He sighed loudly. "My parents are going to kill me if I come home without it!"

"Wait a minute." Nancy was definitely confused by now. "So you're not telling us you wrecked the equipment shed?"

"What? No way!" Eddie said. "I thought Mr. S. said it was the wind."

"Yeah. But everyone thinks it was me," Bess mumbled.

"I don't think that," Eddie told her. "But I definitely didn't do it, either. I didn't even go in the shed after everyone else left. I was planning to look for my backpack in there, but I stepped in some animal poo near the door and I figured I shouldn't go in and get the floor dirty. It was really gross poo, too—black and sort of crumbly looking, and . . ."

"Yuck! Okay, if we want to know more, we'll follow Blizzard around until he poops again." George wrinkled her nose. "So why are you so upset about your backpack, anyway? What's in it—gold and jewels?"

"No, just extra socks and some snacks and comic books for the ride here." Eddie bit his lip. "And my parents' cell phone. That's the reason they'll kill me if I don't find it." He shrugged. "I'm glad we're stuck here overnight.

That gives me more time to look."

"But you didn't know about the avalanche before lunch," Nancy pointed out. "Why didn't you wipe off your shoe and keep searching if you were so worried?"

"I was hungry," Eddie said sheepishly. "I didn't want to miss lunch—especially if my juice box and cheesy crackers were gone forever!"

Just then Eddie's friend Steve came skiing over. Eddie introduced the other boy to the girls. Then the two of them took off to search for Eddie's backpack behind the shed.

"So much for that." Nancy put an X in her notebook next to Eddie's name.

"Are you sure?" George looked over her shoulder. "It's not like he can prove what he just told us."

"I know," Nancy said. "But he seems honest. I have a hunch he's telling the truth."

"I think so too," Bess said. "Some of the other suspects seem way more likely."

"Starting with that one." George was staring off past Nancy and Bess.

Nancy turned around and saw Jack. He was wearing his ski boots, but carrying his skis.

"Hey," Nancy called. "Can we talk to you?"

"I'm kind of busy right now," Jack said in a grouchy voice. "My skis got all messed up when *someone* wrecked the equipment shed." He glared at Bess. "I need to go trade them in for a pair that works right."

His skis *did* look kind of beat up. One had a chip in one end, and there were several long scratches in the other.

George stared at the scratches. "Weird," she whispered to Nancy. "If there was a cat around here, we'd have to add it to our list."

Jack was already continuing on his way. "Come on," Nancy said. "Maybe this is a clue."

They followed Jack into the shed. Mr. Samuels, Henry, and a couple of other Mount Fun employees were inside cleaning up the mess. "Howdy, kids," Mr. Samuels called. "What's up?"

"I need new skis," Jack announced. "These are messed up."

"Help yourself." Mr. Samuels waved toward several sets of kid-size skis lined up against the wall near the door. "We just cleaned up that batch there."

Jack dropped his old skis with the messy ones and walked over to pick out another pair. Nancy followed him.

"Listen," she said. "I know you think Bess messed up the shed. But I know she didn't. I'm just trying to figure out the truth."

Jack shrugged. "Whatever. If she didn't do it, I don't know who did."

Nancy didn't want to make Jack mad. But she had to figure out whether he could have done it. "I saw you at lunch," she said. "You were sitting near the door. Did you leave the room at all?"

"No." Jack glared at her. "And if you don't believe me, you can ask my dad. Or him." He pointed over at Henry. "He was sitting across from me. Why don't you ask him?"

"Um, that's okay." Nancy wandered back to her friends.

"Well?" George said. "Should we go ask Henry?"

"Why bother?" Nancy said. "If Jack was

lying, he wouldn't tell us to ask him." She put an X next to his name too.

"Hey, I found someone's bag," Henry called out. "Does it belong to any of you kids?"

Nancy glanced over and saw the instructor holding up a black backpack. "Nope," she said. "Not ours."

"I recognize that backpack," Jack said. "It belongs to that clumsy kid."

"You mean Eddie?" Bess asked.

Jack nodded. "You know what this means," he exclaimed loudly enough for everyone in the shed to hear. "Eddie's the one who messed up this place!"

ChAPTER EighT

Lost and Found

Eddie appeared in the doorway. "My backpack!" he cried. Henry handed it over, and Eddie started digging through the stuff inside.

Jack crossed his arms. "You might as well confess," he said. "You wrecked the shed, didn't you? What happened, did you trip over your own feet and knock everything over?"

"What?" Eddie said. "I didn't do anything. I haven't seen my backpack in, like, three hours."

He sounded distracted. While he talked, he kept pulling things out of the backpack and tossing them aside. First a pair of gloves, then a couple of empty cheesy cracker wrappers, then a juice box, then a single white sock . . .

He's looking for that cell phone, Nancy thought.

A second later Eddie let out a cry of relief. "It's still here!" he said, holding up a cell phone. Then his smile faded. "Hey," he added. "What's the big idea saying I messed up the shed?"

"You must have done it," Jack said. "How else would your stuff get back there?"

"Kids . . . ," Mr. Samuels began.

"I didn't do it!" Eddie cried. "If you want to know who did it, why don't you ask her?"

He pointed at the doorway. Nancy turned and saw Gina standing there.

"What's going on?" Gina said. "Ask me what?"

"I saw you when I was walking to lunch," Eddie told her. "You were in the hallway near the lobby staring out that big window. If anyone came across the yard to this shed, you would've seen them."

Nancy's eyes widened. Could Gina be about to break the case?

"I didn't see anything," Gina said with a frown. "I was so bored that I was just watching some stupid raccoons playing in the stupid snow over near the stupid benches. There were no people outside the whole time I was looking." She shrugged. "It was probably the stupid wind, like he said." She waved a hand toward Mr. Samuels.

Weird, Nancy thought. *If Gina is telling the truth, how did someone get in here long enough to make this mess without her seeing them? She was out there for at least half of lunchtime.*

"I just realized Gina couldn't have done it," Bess whispered to Nancy. "She didn't have her coat when she ran out of the room, remember? I doubt she'd go outside without it."

Just then George poked Nancy in the arm. "Hey, didn't Eddie say he had some cheesy crackers in his backpack? He must have forgotten he ate them already. Or at least *someone* did." She held up one of the empty wrappers Eddie had tossed out of his bag.

Nancy shrugged. "Maybe there's another package still in there."

She didn't really care about Eddie's cheesy crackers. She was much more interested in what Bess had just remembered about Gina's coat.

So maybe Eddie is the one who's lying, she thought reluctantly. *It does seem strange that his backpack turned up in the middle of the mess.*

"Hey Eddie," George said. "Can I look in your backpack?"

"Sure," Eddie said, handing it over. He was too busy glaring at Jack to ask George why she wanted to look.

George dug into the backpack. She pulled out Eddie's other sock, some comic books, and three more empty cheesy cracker packages.

"Aha!" George said. "I solved the mystery!"

"What do you mean?" Mr. Samuels said.

George smiled

proudly. "It was Blizzard," she announced. "He was trying to get these cheesy crackers. He probably knocked the skis over when he was dragging Eddie's backpack around."

Bess was already shaking her head. "No way," she said. "Blizzard would have eaten the packages, too. Remember? We had to stop him from eating the wrapper from your breakfast bar."

"Oh yeah." George's shoulders slumped. "I thought I had it."

"It wasn't Blizzard. I locked him up during lunch so he wouldn't make a pest of himself begging for food." Mr. Samuels rubbed his mustache, looking worried. "Anyway, why don't you kids let us worry about all this? I just want everyone to have a good time skiing."

He shooed all the kids out of the shed. Nancy and her friends walked out with Eddie.

"That's weird about my crackers," Eddie

said. "I would've sworn I still had, like, three packages left."

"Maybe whoever messed up the shed got hungry and ate them," Nancy said. But she suspected Eddie had eaten the crackers himself and forgotten. Or maybe he'd lost them.

Eddie spotted his friend and hurried off. Nancy, Bess, and George sat down to put on their skis.

Bess sighed. "It feels weird to just ski like nothing happened."

"I know," Nancy said. "But we can keep thinking while we ski. We already know it probably wasn't Jack, or Eddie, or Gina. And it definitely wasn't Blizzard if he was locked up."

"So who else is left?" Bess asked.

Nancy didn't have a good answer to that. And by the time they headed inside for dinner, the Clue Crew hadn't come up with any new suspects. They put their skis away along with everyone else, then met up with George's parents.

"We called home to tell everyone we'd be staying overnight," Mrs. Fayne said as they all walked toward the dining room. "It looks like they won't be able to open the road until tomorrow."

Mr. Fayne chuckled. "Nancy, your father seemed to think you arranged this whole avalanche somehow. He said something about getting out of helping him shovel snow tomorrow morning?"

Nancy smiled weakly. She was distracted by the way at least half the kids in the room turned to stare at them when they stepped into the dining room. Or rather, the way they turned to stare at Bess.

She could tell Bess noticed too. Bess kept her head down as they walked to their table.

We have to clear Bess's name, Nancy thought

with new determination. *We have all night to work on the mystery. And if we can't solve it by tomorrow, we don't deserve to call ourselves the Clue Crew!*

CHAPTER NINE

A Lost Cause?

At dinner, Mr. and Mrs. Fayne ended up chatting with their new friends again. That gave the girls plenty of time to talk about the investigation. But talking about it didn't help much.

"Nobody on our list is a good suspect," Nancy pointed out. "Either they don't have any reason to mess up the shed, like Eddie . . ."

"Or they didn't have the chance to do it, like Jack and Blizzard," George finished.

Bess sighed. "So what do we do now?"

Nancy bit her lip. "Just keep thinking, I guess."

"Here you go," Mr. Samuels said. "The deluxe emergency suite."

He showed the girls and George's parents into one of the lodge's guest rooms. Three cots were squeezed in there along with a double bed.

"Wow," George said. "It's crowded in here."

"Hush," her mother warned. "We're lucky Mr. Samuels was able to fit us in at all."

"True," Mr. Fayne agreed with a chuckle. "But I hope you're giving us the sardine rate, Mr. Samuels."

The lodge owner laughed. "On Kids Weekend, stranded kids stay for half price," he said. "You won't be charged extra for the pj's and toothbrushes my staff scraped up for you to borrow, either."

When Mr. Samuels left, Nancy checked her watch. It was only seven thirty. That left plenty of time for detective work.

"May we go walk around the lodge?" she asked Mrs. Fayne.

Mrs. Fayne checked her watch too. "I don't think so, Nancy," she said. "We'll all have to take turns in the shower. And we want to get to

sleep early. We should leave right after breakfast tomorrow if the road is open by then."

"But Mom . . . ," George began.

"You heard your mother," Mr. Fayne said.
"Who wants the first shower?"

Nancy was disappointed. How were they supposed to solve the mystery if they weren't allowed out of the room?

"Oh well," George whispered to Nancy. "Maybe we can figure it out at breakfast." She yawned.

That started Nancy yawning too. She realized she was tired after the long day of skiing. Maybe going to bed early wasn't such a bad idea after all.

A little over an hour later all five of them were showered, changed, and climbing into bed. Mrs. Fayne turned off the lights. The room still wasn't very dark, though. Bright moonlight reflected off the snow and shone through the window. Within minutes the room was filled with the sounds of deep breathing. But Nancy couldn't seem to fall asleep. She stared at the ceiling and thought about the case. Who could have wrecked the equipment shed? The Clue Crew had started with lots of suspects. But one by one, they had ruled them out. The culprit wasn't Jack; he'd stayed in the dining room all through lunch. It wasn't Eddie; he said he hadn't gone in there, and Nancy believed him. It wasn't Gina, unless she'd gone outside without her coat. And it wasn't Blizzard, because he'd been locked up.

So who did it? Nancy wondered. *Why can't I figure it out?*

She yawned and let her eyes drift shut. If she couldn't solve the mystery, it would be her first real failure as a detective. She didn't like that thought.

But it wasn't enough to keep her awake anymore. At last she fell asleep.

ChaPTER TEN

Aha!

Nancy opened her eyes. For a second she wasn't sure where she was. There were strange shadows on the ceiling and muffled snores all around her.

Then she remembered. She was at the ski lodge.

Her throat felt dry. She sat up and looked around. In the moonlight, she could see everyone else sleeping.

She climbed out of bed, tiptoed to the bathroom, and got a drink of water. Then she headed back toward her cot.

On the way, she paused at the window.

The moon lit up the scene outside as bright as day. Nancy could see the ski lift in the distance and pine trees waving in the breeze on the mountainside.

She also saw something moving below the window. Squinting, she realized it was a family of raccoons—an adult and three youngsters.

Cute! she thought with a smile. She watched as the animals scampered closer to the building. They headed straight for a row of garbage cans.

Through the window, Nancy heard a muffled *thud* as a can hit the ground and the lid popped off. Soon all four raccoons were rummaging through the contents with their little handlike paws.

Nancy's smile widened. She watched the raccoons for a moment longer. Then she slipped back into bed and was asleep as soon as her head hit the pillow.

❀ ❀ ❀

"Okay," George said. "Should we talk about the mystery now?"

In all the commotion of waking up, getting dressed, and packing for the trip home, Nancy and her friends had barely had time to speak.

Now they were sitting at one of the long tables in the dining room having breakfast. Jack and his father were farther down the table, with Gina and her parents across from them. Eddie was at the next table with Steve and his father.

"We don't need to talk about it," Nancy said with a smile. "I solved the case."

"What?" George shrieked. "You mean you figured out who messed up the ski shed?"

All around them, people turned to stare. George blushed. Nancy guessed she hadn't meant to speak so loudly.

But it was too late now. "What?" Eddie called out. "Did you say you know who wrecked the shed?"

"Yes, I think so," Nancy said. "I realized the answer last night."

Mr. Fayne looked confused. "Is this about the vandalism?"

"Yes, Dad," George said. "Everyone still thought Bess did it. So we were trying to clear her name."

Even Mr. Samuels had noticed the commotion. He came over to their table. "Did I hear right?" he asked. "You kids think you know who vandalized my equipment shed?"

"Nancy does," George said. "She didn't tell us yet."

"So spill it!" Gina said impatiently.

Nancy cleared her throat. Everyone was staring at her.

"This was a tough one," she said. "See, there were some people who *could* have done it, but we couldn't see why any of them would *want* to."

She noticed Bess and George sneaking peeks at Eddie. But Nancy didn't mention his name.

"Then there were some who might have *wanted* to do it." She thought about Gina, Jack, and Blizzard. "But none of them had the chance."

"So who did it?" Jack demanded. "The wind?"

"No!" Eddie called out. "I bet it was that dog. He probably wanted my cheesy crackers."

"We thought about that," Nancy said. "But

Blizzard was locked up during lunch." She smiled. "Those cheesy crackers were a good clue, though. They helped me figure it out." She turned to Gina. "I think Gina should be able to figure it out too."

"What?" Gina cried. "You'd better not be accusing me! I didn't even go outside during lunch."

"I know," Nancy said. "But you *did* witness the culprits at the scene of the crime. Just think about it."

Gina kept scowling for a minute. Then she gasped. "Hold on," she cried. "Those raccoons! They did it!"

Mr. Samuels slapped his head. "Of course!" he said. "On such a warm day, raccoons would wake up from hibernation to look for food."

"Yes!" Gina's father spoke up, looking excited. "They did! I noticed lots of raccoon prints in the snow near the shed yesterday afternoon. Droppings, too. Remember, Gina?"

"Ew!" Gina exclaimed. "Dad, don't you ever talk about anything but animal poop?"

Everyone laughed. "Case closed!" Mr. Samuels exclaimed. "Very impressive detective work, young lady."

Nancy glanced around at her friends. "We all helped," she said. "I just finally put the pieces together last night when I saw some raccoons outside. See, they probably came around looking for food while all of us were inside for lunch. They smelled the snacks in our backpacks. Raccoons have those cool fingerlike paws, so they could take the wrappings off the food instead of just eating the whole thing like a dog would. Anyway, Eddie must have dropped his pack inside the shed, and I guess while they were getting out his crackers they knocked over the skis and stuff."

"Hey! My pretzels were missing from my backpack yesterday," a girl called out.

"My apple, too," a boy added. "I thought my brother ate it!"

"The raccoons probably chewed up my mitten," Bess said. "There were crumbs on it from that breakfast bar."

"I must admit, that mitten made me jump to conclusions," Mr. Samuels said. "I'm very sorry to have suspected you, Miss Bess. I should have known our Best New Skier would never do something so rotten."

"It's okay," Bess said shyly.

George glared at Jack. "Aren't you going to apologize too? You kept accusing everyone."

"Whatever," Jack muttered. His father gave him a stern look. "All right, all right," Jack said. He glanced at Bess, and also at Eddie. "Sorry."

Just then Henry ran into the room. He looked confused at seeing everyone huddled around Nancy's table. But he didn't say anything about that.

"Good news, people," he said. "We just got a call that the road is open!"

Nancy cheered along with everyone else.

They had solved the mystery just in time!

"Good news indeed," Mr. Samuels exclaimed. "But I do hope you'll all come back soon. Especially our three talented young detectives." He smiled at Nancy, Bess, and George. "In fact, stop by the lobby on your way out. I want to give you three free day passes for our next Kids Weekend!"

Winter Day Warmth

Nothing is better than hot chocolate after playing in the snow or skiing with your friends. But don't just make it from a packet—your drink should be just as exciting as your day. Homemade hot chocolate is much tastier and fun to create.

Spice Things Up

Did you know the Aztecs in Mexico drank hot chocolate more than four hundred years ago? Their drink was bitter and spicy, until the Spanish came and decided they liked a little sugar with their chocolate. Although Mexican hot chocolate has peppers and other spices, you don't have to make anything that complicated.

You Will Need:

2 egg yolks

2 ounces of a chocolate candy bar (you can use a regular Hershey bar or, for something a little nutty, a Toblerone)

1 cup milk

an adult to help out (and to share the leftovers with)

❀ First, have an adult help you crack the eggs over a large bowl, then beat the yolks with a whisk or a spoon.

❀ Break up the chocolate into small pieces and drop them in a glass measuring cup.

❀ Add milk to the cup and then place it, uncovered, in the microwave. Microwave on medium-high until the chocolate is melted and mixed with the milk—it should take 2 1/2 to 3 minutes.

❀ Pour the milk and chocolate into the bowl with the eggs, then mix everything together thoroughly.

❀ Microwave everything for another minute so it's nice and hot—and then it's ready to drink!

Sugary Sweet!

If your hot chocolate looks too plain, don't forget to add the marshmallows. Some people like to fill their mug with marshmallows and then pour the chocolate over them, while others like to drop in a big scoop of marshmallow fluff and let it float on top. If you want more candy and more color, decorate the floating mound of marshmallow with sprinkles. It's like the opposite of an ice cream sundae . . . perfect for cold days!

Read all the books in the

Blast to the Past

series!